STAR WARS REBELS™

A NEW HERO

WRITTEN BY

PABLO HIDALGO

ILLUSTRATIONS ARE CONCEPT ART DEVELOPED FOR
STAR WARS REBELS BY

THE LUCASFILM
ANIMATION ART DEPARTMENT

DISNEY
LUCASFILM
PRESS

LOS ANGELES • NEW YORK

Copyright © 2014 Lucasfilm Ltd. & ® or TM. All rights reserved. Published by Disney • Lucasfilm Press, an imprint of Disney Book Group. No part of this book may be reproduced or transmitted in any form or by any means, electronic or mechanical, including photocopying, recording, or by any information storage and retrieval system, without written permission from the publisher. For information address Disney • Lucasfilm Press, 1101 Flower Street, Glendale, California 91201.

Printed in the United States of America

First Edition

1 3 5 7 9 10 8 6 4 2

Library of Congress Control Number: 2014937068

ISBN 978-148470669-5

F322-8368-0-14171

Visit www.starwars.com

MY NAME IS EZRA BRIDGER.

I lived alone on the planet Lothal. I know what you're thinking—*Where are his parents?* The truth is I don't know. But that's just fine. I live my life the way I want to. Or try to, anyway. It isn't always easy, and it's gotten a whole lot more complicated lately.

I've lived my whole life on this planet. I know the ins and outs of this world and how to avoid the wrong kinds of attention. These are important things to know, because this planet isn't the easiest place to live on these days.

LOTHAL IS SUCH A TINY SPECK
in such a great big galaxy that it's hard to imagine it being the center of anyone's attention. We're way out on the edge; fly past us and before long you'll run out of galaxy. That's how deep this planet is in the Outer Rim Territories.

This sounds like an astronomy lesson, right? I wouldn't know. I didn't learn my lessons in a classroom. I learned everything I know from the spacers who come into town and from overhearing people talk in the marketplaces. I've taught myself what I need to survive by keeping my eyes and ears open.

Most of Lothal is just seemingly endless grasslands. The most excitement you'll find in these parts is a Loth-cat chasing down a Loth-rat for a quick snack. Walk far enough and you'll see the grasslands broken up by huge old stones sticking straight up from the ground. Where these rocks crowd together makes a good place to hide and lie low. Remember that, because it's good to have hiding places these days.

In the grasslands, farmers and ranchers make a living through hard, honest work. They're good people, but I've never been one for farming.

Capital City is where you'll find the most people on this world. It's where people run the businesses of Lothal. Besides farming, this planet's business is in minerals. Lothal is lucky enough to have a trove of valuable gems and ores in its rock. But it's also *unlucky*, because that's what drew the Galactic Empire here.

When they think it's safe and no Imperials are listening, the old pilots at the spaceport talk about a time when there wasn't an Empire. I don't know anything about that. Seems to me the Imperials have always been around. But lately they've become a lot harder to ignore. Even out in the grasslands, where there's nothing around, you might see Imperial ships soar by.

YOU ALWAYS HEAR THEM FIRST.
Twin ion engines make TIE fighters howl as they fly by
on patrols, looking for trouble. I'm too small to show
up on their scopes, and that's fine by me.

The city is filling up with soldiers in white armor. They call themselves **STORMTROOPERS**, and the Empire uses them to keep order on Lothal. They say they're here to protect us. What they're really here to protect are the factories, farms, and mines—to profit the Empire. They don't care about Lothal, or the people who work hard. They only care about what they're taking *out* of Lothal.

What makes it worse is that, underneath those white stormtrooper helmets and black TIE fighter pilot helmets, a lot of the Imperials actually come from here. There are training academies set up now that turn good Lothal folks into soldiers of the Empire.

I guess a lot of people here, being so used to living out on the edge of nowhere, signed up because they wanted to connect to something bigger. Can't they see what they're signing up for?

The Empire only wants power. It's the biggest bully in the galaxy. It wants to tell people how to live and what to think. And if you disagree with the Empire, you disappear. No one is safe. So people on Lothal just go through their days, pretending that life is okay and normal, even though they're really afraid.

Imperial ships keep appearing in the skies over Lothal. Somebody in the Empire has decided that Lothal and its minerals are worth guarding. Huge Star Destroyers—ships bigger than you can imagine—fly overhead. You can't help feeling small against ships that big.

And you certainly don't feel safe.

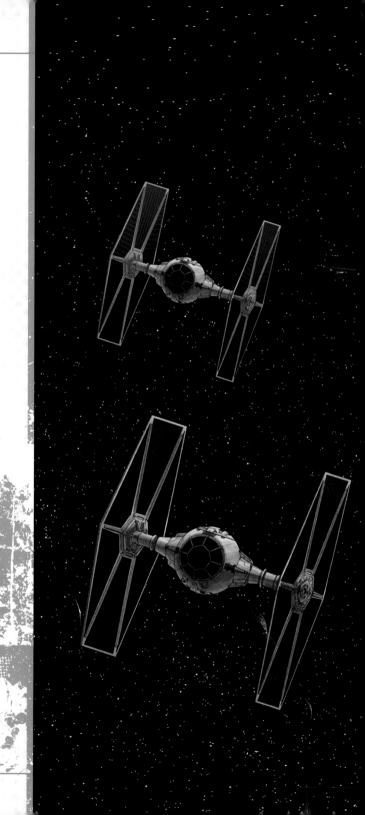

Me, I avoided the Empire by living outside Capital City. I've made myself a little roost at the top of an old communications tower. These towers used to serve a purpose here. They were used to guide the few visitors who came to Lothal to the spaceports. That was before the Empire. Now the Empire controls most of the traffic in and out, and it has left these old towers empty. That's how Imperial progress works. Throw away the old. I won't let this one go to waste, though.

From here, I can see Capital City. I can see the smoke coughed out by the factories where a lot of Lothal people work, slaving away to make more and more TIE fighters for the Empire. It's hard to imagine a worse way to spend a beautiful Lothal day. It's easier to imagine what Lothal might have been like if its people hadn't been so quick to let the Empire settle here.

I can imagine what this planet might be like without the Empire, with people who weren't afraid all the time and didn't have anyone breathing down their necks.

I thought I was the only one who thought like that. I thought nobody would be brave enough to take the fight to the Empire. It'd be hopeless, right? Countless Imperial troops, endless TIE fighters, and warships that can fill up the sky—who would dare to take a stand against all that?

Sometimes the galaxy finds just the right mix of crazy and brave. That's where my new friends come in. I didn't know they were out there, trying to do right. They flew around in their starship, the *Ghost*, doing what they could to rebel against the Empire. From slowing down Imperial cargo ships to stealing Imperial supplies, the crew of the *Ghost* specialized in making things a lot more complicated for the Empire.

When I met them, they were a tight-knit crew of five, each with their own grudge against the Empire. They all have their own strengths and can fight together like a team. Keeping a low profile is important to them. They operate with code names like Spectre-1 and Spectre-2 so the Empire can't find out their true identities. I can appreciate that. With the Empire around, you have to keep some secrets.

Their ship's name, the *Ghost*, and their Spectre code names reflect how they operate. They strike quickly and then vanish. The Empire can feel their presence but can't grab them before they disappear. Maybe it's time for the Imperials to feel spooked for a change.

I've been on my own for most of my life. I survive on the streets by taking what I need. I'm not hurting anyone, just the Empire and its stooges. Besides, the Empire's not going to miss a few scraps of food and the odd piece of tech.

I made the mistake of thinking there were some new stooges in town. They didn't look like they were from Lothal, which fit my plans. I figured if they were leaving the planet soon, they wouldn't waste too much time chasing down a street kid who nicked a bit of their cargo. They probably had bigger, brighter places to be than Lothal, after all.

That's what I was thinking when I stole from them. It's what I do best, but that day I guess I wasn't at my best, because I forgot one of my most important rules.

Not to lecture you, but one of Ezra Bridger's most important rules of life on the streets of Lothal is this: Looks can be deceiving. I count on that. That's why the Empire is always underestimating me. I'm not what it thinks. I'm not just a street kid who's afraid of a stormtrooper like everyone else on Lothal is. When people assume that, they turn their backs on me and let down their guard. But that day in the marketplace, I was the one doing the underestimating. I misjudged this crew.

I noticed that they were thieves like me. Their supplies were stolen from the Empire. I knew because I had been eyeing the goods. It turned out they had no intention of keeping the loot for themselves. No, this crew was going to give away those stolen Imperial supplies (Can you imagine that? Just give them away!) to the poor farmers of Lothal that the Empire had pushed around. I didn't see that coming, and I'm usually pretty good at seeing things coming.

So while Imperial stormtroopers were chasing them, this crew started chasing me to get back what I'd stolen. I guess I made a memorable first impression.

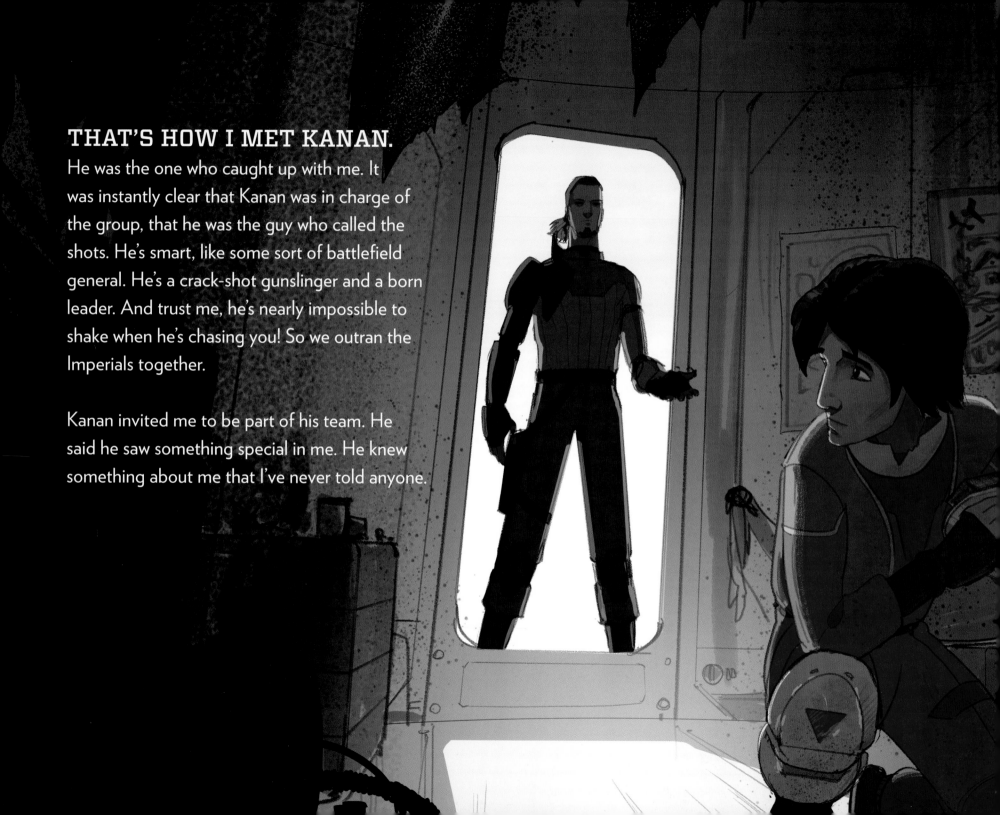

THAT'S HOW I MET KANAN.

He was the one who caught up with me. It was instantly clear that Kanan was in charge of the group, that he was the guy who called the shots. He's smart, like some sort of battlefield general. He's a crack-shot gunslinger and a born leader. And trust me, he's nearly impossible to shake when he's chasing you! So we outran the Imperials together.

Kanan invited me to be part of his team. He said he saw something special in me. He knew something about me that I've never told anyone.

The truth is sometimes I can see things before they happen. It's not like clear pictures or in ways I can describe. . . . It's like my body knows what's going to happen next and moves me out of the way. Kanan knew I could do this. He told me it's because I can sense something called the FORCE.

Once aboard the *Ghost*, I met Kanan's crew. I've never seen a better pilot than **HERA**. The *Ghost* is her ship and she knows every bolt and plate of it. She's great at getting us out of trouble, which I'm quickly finding out happens a lot!

She's a Twi'lek from the planet Ryloth. I hear the Empire hasn't been too kind to Ryloth, so I figure that's why she's fighting back. Though, now that I think of it, she doesn't talk much about her past, or herself. Hera seems more interested in finding out how others are doing, and how she can help. That took some getting used to.

This junky little astromech droid keeps the *Ghost* running. Lucky for him he's good at it, because he is a pain. His name is **CHOPPER**, and he's a patched-together, creaky-jointed antique. He's always cranky about something and bleeps and blarps his complaints nonstop. They don't pull out his batteries because he's useful. The *Ghost* is so modified and powered up that it needs an expert to keep it in top shape, and Chopper's the one to do it.

SABINE is the weapons expert of the team. She's a real know-it-all and not afraid to show it. She's an artist, and that's someone you don't meet every day on Lothal. She's really talented, too. It's like the Empire wants to paint over everything with its boring shades of gray, black, and white. Sabine puts the color back. I think TIE fighters look a lot better after one of her paint bombs has gone off.

Yeah, I guess you can say I really admire her. That is, I admire her work. Let's be clear: she's gifted. I mean, anyone with a good eye would say so, right? I have no idea what she thinks of me. Not that I care. . . . Anyway, let's move on to Zeb.

ZEB is the muscle of the group. He's great at smashing things, including things he doesn't mean to smash. He's good to have in a fight, but he gets carried away. For a tall guy, he's got a short temper—which is why it's so much fun to get him going. Chopper and I take turns seeing who can get him riled up the most. Are all Lasat this touchy? I don't know because I've never seen another Lasat. It turns out not many people have.

freighter, going about its business of moving cargo from one star system to another. But remember that Ezra Bridger lesson about looks being deceiving? On the inside, the *Ghost* has many surprises.

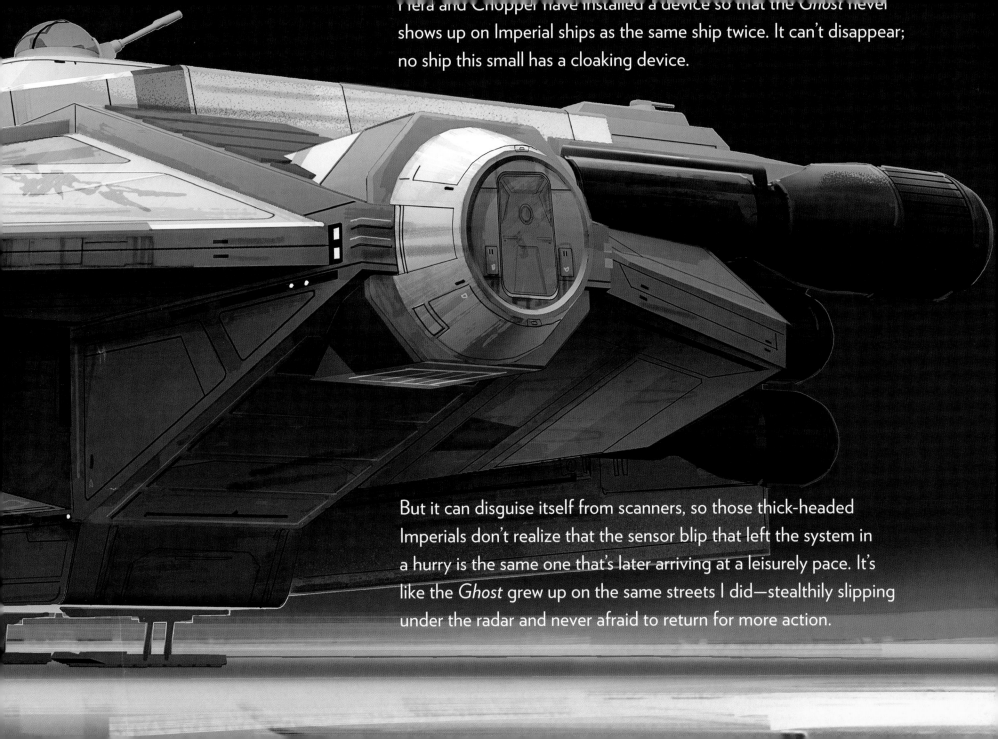

Hera and Chopper have installed a device so that the *Ghost* never shows up on Imperial ships as the same ship twice. It can't disappear; no ship this small has a cloaking device.

But it can disguise itself from scanners, so those thick-headed Imperials don't realize that the sensor blip that left the system in a hurry is the same one that's later arriving at a leisurely pace. It's like the *Ghost* grew up on the same streets I did—stealthily slipping under the radar and never afraid to return for more action.

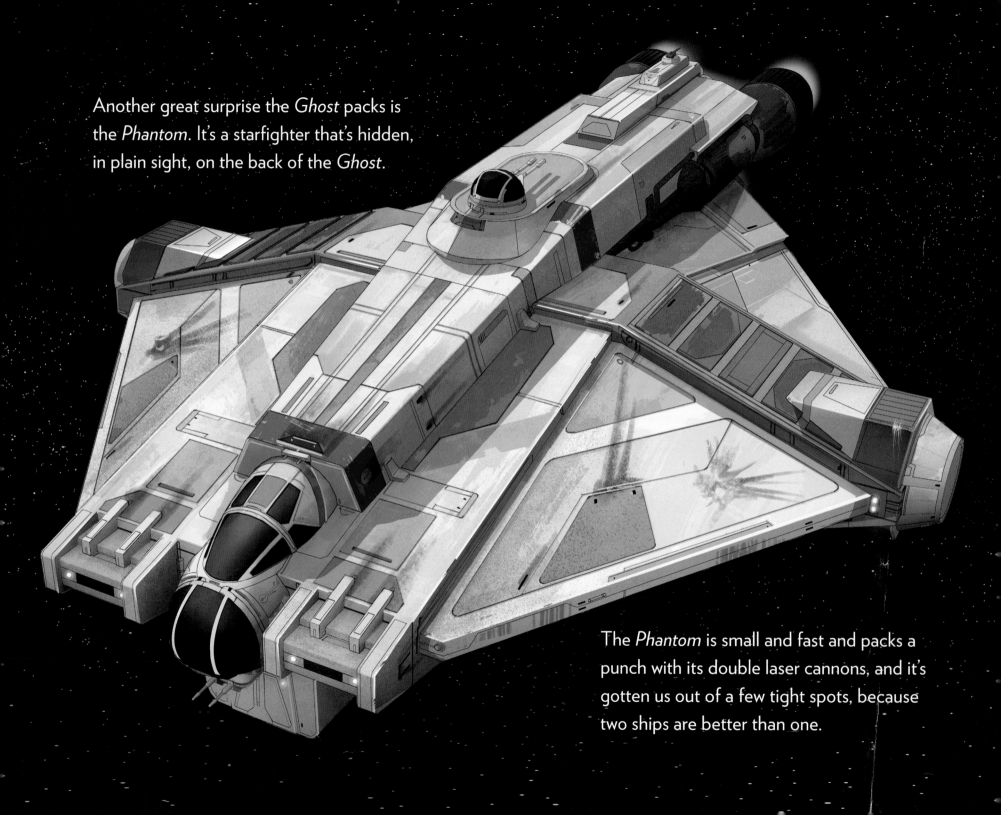

Another great surprise the *Ghost* packs is the *Phantom*. It's a starfighter that's hidden, in plain sight, on the back of the *Ghost*.

The *Phantom* is small and fast and packs a punch with its double laser cannons, and it's gotten us out of a few tight spots, because two ships are better than one.

I had never before been in space until that day Kanan brought me aboard the *Ghost*. Now I can't imagine life without outrunning or outshooting Imperial TIE fighters. Maybe someday I'll get a chance to pilot us out of trouble.

I'll admit it: it took me a while to get used to operating with a team. You've got to remember, on Lothal I worked alone. So on our first mission together, which involved freeing Wookiee prisoners from the Empire, there were times I was thinking about myself first. It's what had always kept me alive and out of Imperial hands, after all.

I thought the crew of the *Ghost* would leave me behind on Lothal when we finished our mission. I needed to make sure I got something worthwhile for my troubles. I figured that laser sword that Kanan carried would fetch a few credits or maybe come in handy in a scrap. So I took it.

Kanan knew. But he wasn't mad. Getting mad is not the Jedi way.

See, I found out that Kanan is a Jedi.
JEDI KNIGHTS were guardians
of peace and justice before the Empire
nearly wiped all of them out. And now it's
a very dangerous time to be a Jedi, but
Kanan is one because the galaxy needs
people to fight for those who can't. He
can feel the Force, a mystical energy field
that connects all living things in the galaxy.

Kanan says I can feel it, too. He says he
can train me in the ways of the Force to
become a Jedi and become connected to
something far bigger than Lothal, bigger
than the Empire, bigger than anything I
can imagine.

I accepted Kanan's offer and returned his lightsaber. Now I'm part of the team. Life moves pretty fast with this crew. We're always blasting off on a new adventure, helping those who need it, keeping the *Ghost* fueled, and letting the Empire know it can't push everyone around. I'm now Spectre-6 and part of what is, basically, a unique kind of family.

We stay near Lothal, because the Empire wants it and its people need our help. I'm fast on my feet and small enough to squeeze into and out of trouble spots. And like Kanan said, I've got the Force. And I'm learning to use it.

WHICH BRINGS ME TO THE INQUISITOR.

See, most Imperials aren't worth getting scared about. That's part of what our crew does best: we show the people of Lothal that they don't need to be afraid of stormtroopers, or TIE fighter pilots, or bumbling Imperial officers. They can stand up for themselves and what's right.

But the Inquisitor . . . the Inquisitor is *scary*. I think he even scares Kanan.

When the Empire came to power, it went to a lot of effort to wipe out all the Jedi Knights. The Empire does not want any Jedi interfering with its plans. The Inquisitor is the Imperial agent whose job it is to hunt down and destroy all Jedi. Or even any Jedi in training. Lucky me, right?

THE INQUISITOR HAS THE FORCE,

too, but he's not a Jedi. Kanan explained that the Inquisitor uses the power of the dark side. He uses hate, fear, and anger to become more powerful, and he carries a lightsaber, too. Kanan tells me not to be afraid and not to be angry. It's hard, but he explains that to be a Jedi is to trust in the Force. To trust that it will guide you, and to trust that you will use it well.

I have to remember that. It's easy to think that you're too small. That the Empire is too big. But the Force is limitless. It's bigger than the whole galaxy, and the Empire couldn't crush the power of the Jedi though it tried its hardest.

Because Kanan and I are still around.

We're here to stay, no matter what the Empire throws at us. We'll always keep fighting until the Empire leaves Lothal alone. We'll keep helping people who aren't strong or brave enough to help themselves. We work as a team, and we're stronger for it. Kanan leads the way. Zeb clears all obstacles. Hera gets us out of danger. Sabine leaves our mark. Chopper keeps us running.

Me, I'm keeping my eyes and ears open and helping my team find the ins and outs of Lothal. I'm using everything I learned on the streets, and all that I'm starting to learn from Kanan about the Force, to make a far bigger difference than I could have made by myself.

So don't be afraid of the Empire. Believe in something bigger than it. Believe in yourself.